AUGUSTA
& TRAB

AUGUSTA
& TRAB

by Christopher de Vinck

FOUR WINDS PRESS ❖ NEW YORK
MAXWELL MACMILLAN CANADA • TORONTO
MAXWELL MACMILLAN INTERNATIONAL
NEW YORK • OXFORD • SINGAPORE • SYDNEY

Acknowledgments
The poem in the last chapter is titled "To Maria."
The poem comes from my mother's
book, *A Time To Gather*.
A Time To Gather
Copyright © Catherine de Vinck, 1967
Alleluia Press, Allendale, New Jersey

Four Winds Press
Macmillan Publishing Company
866 Third Avenue
New York, NY 10022
Maxwell Macmillan Canada, Inc.
1200 Eglinton Avenue East
Suite 200
Don Mills, Ontario M3C 3N1
Macmillan Publishing Company is part of the Maxwell
Communication Group of Companies.
First edition
Printed and bound in the United States of America

10   9   8   7   6   5   4   3   2   1
The text of this book is set in 14-point Garamond ITC Bk.
Book design by Christy Hale

Library of Congress Cataloging-in-Publication Data
de Vinck, Christopher, date.
Augusta & Trab / by Christopher de Vinck.—1st ed.
p.   cm.
Summary: A year after her mother's death,
ten-year-old Augusta and her cat, Trab,
set out on a fanciful journey that helps Augusta
come to terms with her loss.
ISBN 0-02-729945-7
[l. Death—Fiction.   2. Cats—Fiction.]   I. Title.
PZ7.D4977Au   1993
[Fic]—dc20   93-7897

To David, Karen, and Michael

Contents

My sweetness is to wake in the night after days of dry heat, hearing the rain.

—WENDELL BERRY

1

The Peach Tree

If you think enough fanciful thoughts something good is bound to happen. One night I thought very hard that a peach tree would grow in our back lot under the moonlight and that the next day I would pick the fruit and bake a pie. I like the crust.

The next morning I wanted to tell my father about the peach tree. He's a veterinarian. He doesn't charge people much money for taking care of their animals, and he is very busy. (I could tell he didn't have time for breakfast because his coffee mug was still in the cupboard.)

When I saw his mug in the cupboard, I knew it was going to be another empty day, so I grumbled a bit, kicked open the back door, and ran outside. Trab, my cat, came along, too.

We have no garden behind our house, and I really didn't know what a peach tree looked like, and all that I saw patiently waiting for me was a single stem of weak yarrow.

Trab always says to look for the good in everything, so he and I ran out to examine the weed. I took my roller skates, just in case, and Trab brought his bell. You can never tell when an adventure might pop up at you like a jack-in-the-box.

As we ran out the kitchen door, I could see the grayish flower swaying in a crack of the old cement. There wasn't much else to see except broken glass, an old tire I roll around in sometimes, the gray walls of the next building, a brown color in the air, and the usual shadows.

Trab reached the wildflower first, smelling it once, then sitting still as a statue, except for his tail, which swayed back and forth behind him like a woolly snake.

It was a bit awkward running with my roller skates in my hand. It was even more difficult not to cry out with disappointment when I stood before the flower. I was hoping to eat a juicy peach on that hot morning.

Disappointment always leaves in my mouth an empty taste for honey. Whenever I don't get what I want, at least there is always honey. It makes my mouth sweet and my thoughts slippery; then I usually sing.

2

Trab

The flower was small, each floret like a button, but yarrow just the same—a flower. I asked Trab whether we should pick it. All he said was, "Mystery! Mystery! Mystery!"

Until I met Trab at the park gate, I didn't believe animals could talk, although I always wished that they could, because they always seem to be listening, especially cats.

One particular Saturday afternoon, I ran to the park. On that day I was full of honey because I had just come back from my mother's funeral. My mother had been sick for a long time.

A few days before she died, when she was in her bed, she pressed my hand against her cheek and said she would always be with me. I asked her if she could come to my spring concert at school. "I will be there," she said. Then she kissed my hand.

When she died two days later I began to feel a space growing inside me. My mother wouldn't be at my concert, and I didn't get a chance to give her the perfumed soap I made for her in school.

My mother loved perfume, and wood boxes, wildflowers, and plants on the windowsill. She loved me, too. That is what we'd tell each other, but not with any great show like balloons or cupcakes. Our love was more like bread from the oven: warm, full of soft insides, and a thin crust all around glazed with butter. That's how we were: bakers in the kitchen.

I didn't know who to say all this to after

the funeral, so I ate lots of honey and ran out through the back door to the park. After singing a few church songs to myself, I shouted to this old cat licking its paws as it sat beside the iron gate at the park entrance: "I bet *you* don't like bread!" Then I sat down on the grass and cried.

Well, Trab isn't the type of cat to lick your face, but right then and there he told me he did indeed like bread, especially with jam evenly spread across the top, and not along the edges. This stopped my crying, not because Trab talked but because, just like me, he, too, doesn't like jam slipping over the sides of his bread.

"It's hard to hold a jam sandwich if the sides are sticky," Trab said as I looked up from the grass. "And besides, what is the use in talking to you if you are only going to make a fuss and not do anything?"

"But what should I do?" I asked.

"Do? The park. Perhaps you could run in the park. Do you like the park?"

"Yes. It always tells me things, like how to listen. I counted twelve different birds one afternoon just by listening to their different singing."

"Well, just the same I like your singing," Trab said, suddenly standing on all his feet and stretching.

"But I wasn't singing," I said.

"You weren't listening properly," Trab answered as he rubbed against my leg. "Take me home."

So I picked Trab up in my arms, pressed his right paw against my cheek, and then carried him home.

That's how I met Trab. That was last year. I'm ten now, but sometimes I pretend I'm eighty. No one can really tell I'm pretending, especially when I speak in a low voice like this: "I am delighted you could come. Won't you sit down?"

Mrs. Coster down the street *is* eighty. I stop at her house on the way home from school on her baking day. She lives alone. Her house is old and tall, and there is a basket on the front door where you can leave her notes or flowers.

Her cheeks feel round and soft when I kiss them. She makes gingerbread cookies in the shapes of different animals every Thursday morning. All day in school I know those animals are there waiting for me—giraffes, elephants, rabbits, turtles.

Trab is usually my guest when I play eighty. He sits nicely on the couch and listens while I tell him all the neighborhood gossip: how Patricia Plumbird lost a feather, or how Glass-in-the-Window doesn't like to have all those bees and flies bumping into her all day.

When you pretend that you are eighty you have to walk in black shoes and lower your head a great deal. Trab said I look like someone who has lost a penny.

3

Wishes and the Music Box

"Trab," I said, pretending to be a gardener, "make a wish and I'll pick the flower."

"I'd like a jungle!"

Trab always wished for a jungle before I blew out my birthday candles, or when the moon squeezed her way down our alley and poked her nose through our window. We both like to make wishes in the moonlight.

"I'd like a jungle with many orange tigers, and fat lions, and a panther or two who would call upon me for advice on the best ways to keep safe in the dark. I would be very good at telling those beasts how to get around in the world." Trab likes to brag.

I told Trab he could wish for his silly jungle, but I was going to wish for a commission in the Queen's Royal Navy, because I read once about a queen who protected her entire kingdom from all her enemies after she built many beautiful ships with white linen sails. Ever since reading that book, I wanted to travel, especially on a sailing ship, and especially on the ocean.

I don't know why I like the ocean. Once, when I was three, my mother brought me to the beach, and I cried and cried and cried. The waves thumped down on the sand, which reminded me of a dream I kept having of long, white fingers bubbling up from the blue water, grabbing my legs, and slowly dragging me into the surf.

I didn't cry because I was afraid, but

because my mother wouldn't let me take my music box to the beach. My music box is not the type of thing you'd want to leave behind. The bottom is made of brown wood. On the sides, painted stars and moons dance every which way. On top sits a tall glass dome. When the key is wound up, a swan turns around and around along the outer edge inside the dome. In the center, a boy and a girl sit on a bench under an umbrella. When the key is turned, the umbrella spins. The music box plays a tune that goes something like this: "La, la, la! La, la, la! Trink, trink, trink, trink! La, la, la! La, la, la! Trinka, trinka, trink!"

My mother gave me this box on the day I was born. She said that when I was little, I liked to watch the swan and umbrella spin around just before I went to sleep.

4

A Root and a Key

I reached down to pick the flower, but it would not break free. I pulled and pulled and pulled until Trab began to laugh. Then I, too, began to laugh, though my hand hurt from all that pulling.

"Give it a last tug, but this time pretend you are a dentist," Trab suggested.

"But, Trab, I've never pretended to be a dentist before."

"Oh bother, just sound medical. Lean over the patient. Ask it to open wide."

"Good morning, plant."

"*Pisst*," Trab whispered. "I think it is a lady."

"Good morning, Miss Plant. Let me see how you are feeling today." The green leaves seemed to separate a bit.

"That's it, Augusta. Get on with it. Be a dentist. Be a dentist." Trab likes to get his way.

With both my hands firmly around the stem, I pulled and pulled and pulled again until I felt some motion underground. I pulled some more. The flower moved up a bit, then a little more and a little more. I gave a final tug, which freed not only the flower but also the root. Tied to the end of this root was a key. Not a typical key: It had pumpkin teeth on one end, and the other end was in the shape of a heart. The key was blue.

"That doesn't look like a jungle!" Trab meowed.

"And it doesn't very much look like a commission in the Queen's Royal Navy," I said. "But just the same, it's not something ordinary. What do you suppose this key opens?"

I had found lots of keys in my short life. When I stuck my hand under the couch pillows while looking for dimes one afternoon, I found a dirty brown key that must have come with the couch when it arrived from the thrift shop. I also found a peach pit and a silver whistle, so I always thought that the couch once belonged to a policeman who liked peaches.

I also found, once on my way home from school, a key attached to a little ring with an iron monkey swinging from the chain. I kept the monkey and threw the key away. I don't like keeping a key that doesn't belong to a lock. It's like the goose eggs we keep on our living room shelf. They have a little hole on each end where the insides were blown out, leaving the empty shells. I always thought it strange to keep an egg with nothing in it.

You cannot throw away a lock because it is usually attached to a door, but a lost key is light and free, easy to pitch over a fence. This blue key was different: I didn't want to throw it away. I had to find out where it belonged. I untied it from the root and dropped it into my pocket. I gave the flower to Trab, who tossed it around as if it were a large-headed snake about to strike. Then Trab and I decided to go roller skating.

5

Stirring Up the Dust

The first thing I do when we decide to roller skate is to fetch the straw broom from under the back steps and sweep a clear, smooth area in the back lot. I ran to get the broom while Trab tried to pull off the bell from around his neck. As soon as I returned, I began sweeping a circle in the lot.

I swept and swept. Suddenly, a cloud of dust grew and grew until I couldn't see. The dust was thick and brown and gray. I heard

Trab's little bell ringing and ringing. It sounded far off. Then slowly the dust began to settle, and the more it did, the more I could see. And the more I could see, the more I saw a tall, strange shape standing before me. It was a tree, a peach tree, a tall peach tree with plump pink peaches at the tip of each branch; a peach tree with a tall skinny door in the trunk. And on the door was a sign in blue paint: KEEP THIS DOOR LOCKED AT ALL TIMES.

"I don't think we are going roller skating today, Trab," I said as I looked and looked at the new tree standing in the middle of the freshly swept circle. "How do you suppose this happened?"

"I always tell you not to sweep so hard," Trab answered. "You stir things up too much each time. Now look what you've done!"

I walked up to the tree, picked a peach, and sucked the juice out of each mouthful before swallowing.

"Trab," I asked, "do you think it would be rude to knock on the door? After all, no one invited us."

"Well," Trab said, curling his tail, "no one invited the tree here either, so I guess we're even. You may as well use your blue key."

That is what I did. I dug into my pocket and . . . between a stick of peppermint and my lucky penny, I found the key. I approached the tree trunk, which seemed to lean forward, and jiggled the key into the keyhole of the tall, thin door.

"Trab, do you think I should turn the key to the left or to the right?"

But Trab didn't answer. He just sat there, looking at me, turning his head from side to side.

6

The Doorman

I took a chance, and turned the key to the left. I heard a small *click,* and then a *tick-tock;* then the door swallowed my key.

I suppose I should have been afraid, and I would have been if I wasn't so worried about Trab, who ran through the door and disappeared. But then I *was* frightened when a very tall man in a navy blue coat with gold braid on his shoulders stepped out from behind the door and screamed:

"Keep this door locked! Didn't you see the sign?"

"Is that any way to speak to someone you just met?" I snapped, stepping back at a safe distance.

"You were told to keep your pockets empty, and now you have taken everything away!"

"My pockets? No one said anything about pockets!"

"Oh," said the man in blue, dropping his shoulders. "You are the wrong little girl. But the sign does say to keep the door locked, and here you are with roller skates in your hand and the door open wide as a cave."

"But what harm can that do? Doors are made to be opened."

"It depends upon the type of door."

"Well," I was quick to answer, "I did have the right key."

"Yes, you did. That does mean something. Very well. Watch your step. The gangplank is narrow. If you fall into the water, don't blame me!"

With that said, the man in blue gave me a proper salute, winked, and said, "Try not to disappear."

I turned to ask him just what he meant, but *he* had disappeared. I was ready to step back through the door. I was even ready to go home to bed, but the door was no longer there behind me, and besides, I had to find Trab.

Try not to disappear? Try not to disappear? Could he have meant into the water? I thought. As I looked down, I saw my reflection staring back at me. I waved, and the girl in the water waved back. Then I heard a new voice.

7

The Captain

Navigation! Navigation, my girl! Nothing but navigation!"

I turned toward the narrow plank, which led to a tall ship with huge white sails. Standing on the far deck was a man wearing a red coat and a feathered hat. I could see his brass buttons, the gold stripes running along the legs of his pants, and his beard.

"What?" I asked.

"Navigation! All it takes is a few careful steps through the middle, and you'll be able to cross without any trouble."

"The middle?"

"The gangplank," the captain said irritably. "The boarding piece. Grab hold of a star. Step out of yourself, and come aboard."

"Should I bring my skates?" I asked, wishing I had my suitcase filled with a clean dress, a hat or two, my raincoat, and pajamas.

"What you bring is for your entertainment," said the man of the sea. "Come aboard! Come aboard! The gale's up, and changing direction. Let's fly! Let's fly!"

I held my skates, one in each hand for balance, and walked slowly along the thin board until I reached the ship's rail.

"I like your boat," I called up to the captain, hoping a compliment would improve my welcome. By now, I could no longer turn back.

"You like my *what*!" the captain roared.

"Your boat. I like your boat."

"My dear girl. If you see the moon, you do not flatter him by calling him a charming dot in the night sky. If a flower bends toward you as you pass through the garden, you would not sniff and say, 'How much *like* perfume!' Say what you mean, and with the proper word, or say nothing!"

With that, my host turned away, walked up a thin flight of stairs, and stood behind a great wheel.

It did not take me long to realize I had insulted him, for the closer I looked, the more I realized that this was far more than a boat. It was beautiful, in a spinning wheel sort of way, held together with many ropes looped between two tall masts.

I had seen ships in my picture books, but nothing like this one: all brass and wood and fine white sails. The rails arched back and forth. The deck looked like the palm of my father's hand: smooth and wrinkled in spots.

It was an old ship, not weather-beaten but weather-worn like driftwood: silver-colored, soft and light. What I liked best was how I felt when I first placed my feet firmly on the deck: at home.

This feeling of comfort encouraged me to ask the captain about my first concern: "Have you seen Trab, my cat?"

I noticed the wind was beginning to swirl. Waves began to crash against the bow. Ropes slapped against the mast, so I had to yell again through my cupped hands: "Sir? Have you seen Trab?"

The captain gave a tug at his beard, as if he were thinking, then said with great authority, "Augusta, step forward please."

I was puzzled about this request because it sounded like a whisper, a wind voice, but there I saw the captain at his wheel waving me forward. I was so puzzled about how the captain could whisper in my ear from so far off that at first I didn't notice that he knew my name, and I forgot completely that he had not answered my question about Trab.

8

The Commission

How did you know my name?" I asked as I climbed the thin stairs and stood to the captain's right.

"Oh, it's written on the commission. Ah, somewhere here." He let go of the wheel and began searching deep inside the pockets of his red coat.

"Let me see. Ah, no. What's this?"

The captain pulled out a map, a fish, a bell.

"Now, if you'll just wait a second," he said.

As the captain fumbled in his pockets, the ship's wheel began to spin, causing the deck to rock back and forth.

"Somewhere, a commission, the latest one. Your name? Ah. Here!"

He pulled out a neatly rolled paper with a gold ribbon tied around the middle.

"It's from the queen, you know. All very proper! Shall I read it to you?"

"Yes, please do!" I answered, curious to know how a queen could have possibly known who I was.

The captain stood up, cleared his throat, and read:

Be it in my power to dictate my wishes from this humble spot under divine authority: I here do decree it is my prayer and will that one Augusta be escorted to any port or cloud of her choosing. Commissioned here and dated, too.

The Queen

"You are Augusta?" the captain asked, looking up from his paper.

"Yes," I said quietly.

"So what will it be then: port or cloud?"

"What did you say?" I asked, not really understanding.

"The commission, Augusta. Where would you like to go?"

"Well . . ." I thought a moment. "I'd like to see the world, if I may."

"I can give you the world in a bucket, to be cast overboard and mingled with the sea, or I can give it to you one drop at a time. What do you prefer?"

"How strong is your ship?" I asked, not wanting to add any nicks or dents to the already battered hull.

"The shadow of this lady has crossed many harbors: Bombay, Hong Kong...Never over-estimate your obstacles, Augusta. So, port or cloud?"

"Port," I said. "I'd like to see the world one drop at a time."

"So port it is," the captain answered with sudden energy. He grasped the wild wheel, turned the ship around, and headed west.

9

Chocolate

I wish I could say that I felt secure with the way things were turning out. After all, I was on an official ship of the Royal Navy. The trouble was I wasn't quite sure which Royal Navy, and I did not see a crew. Most ships I dreamed about had at least a cabin boy, a cook, and a few rough men with drooping mustaches and crooked daggers. I was beginning to wish I was back home. Which reminded me. Where was Trab?

The wind was twice the strength of fifty fans. The waves leaped up like heavy blankets. The sails expanded like giant balloons. The captain was leaning forward in the gale. I pressed my hands to my ears, hoping the wild wind would simply go away, when I felt something tugging at my leg.

"Augusta!" Trab's calm voice and gentle pawing brought back some of the courage I had abandoned to the storm. "Augusta, I'm hungry . . . and we are being followed."

"Trab! Where have you been?" I asked between screaming gusts of wind.

"Have you got any supper in your pockets?"

"I only have a piece of peppermint," I replied, trying to stand on the rolling deck.

"But, Augusta, we are miles away from a restaurant, and I don't like peppermint. Haven't you a mouse, a bowl of milk, some chocolate perhaps?"

I can explain why Trab likes chocolate.

His father used to lick the bowl after the cook of his house prepared the cake batter, and, as Trab explained, Trab's father always returned home on those cake days with his whiskers evenly coated with chocolate mix. When he kissed Trab good-night, some of the smooth, dark sweetness brushed against Trab's face, and he licked the chocolate off his father's whiskers before going to sleep.

I know, too, that Trab asks for chocolate whenever he is afraid. I thought he was concerned about the growing storm. I didn't know he was actually frightened by the unexpected guest who was following us.

"Trab, all I have is a peppermint. Your dinner is on the middle shelf in the cupboard, but at the moment I've misplaced the cupboard and the whole neighborhood."

"But, Augusta . . ." Trab began to say when he, the captain, the dancing ship, and I rose up into the air with a tremendous rush of wind and water; then we all crashed down again.

With courage and experience, the captain held his ground behind the wheel. I was lying flat on the deck. Trab was on top of me, whispering in my ear, "I really wish I had some chocolate."

10

The Giant Whale

Captain!" I shouted with as much bravery as I could gather. "Do you think we are in danger?"

"Nonsense, girl! Danger is letting go. Lowering the flags."

"Well," Trab cut in, "ask him if ships have tails."

"What did you say, Trab?"

"Ask him if ships have tails. Go on, ask him."

"Captain!" I shouted. "Do ships have tails?"

The wind grew into a monster. Water rose above the sails; soon we were to be swallowed up into the deep.

"A tail, did you say?" the captain screamed back.

"Say, 'Yes,' Augusta," I heard Trab shout.

"Yes! Do ships have tails?"

"A stern, Augusta. Not a tail, a stern!"

"Augusta!" Trab yelled. "Look behind the captain. Behind the captain!"

I focused my eyes through the thick mist of water and wind. And there, beyond the captain, sticking out from the rear of the ship, was an enormous black tail that, indeed, looked as if it were part of the hull.

I knew the seas belonged to monsters. I had seen pictures of great jellylike creatures swallowing innocent ships. I had heard about Jonah. But nothing prepared me for the size of that tail, which must have belonged to the world's greatest whale. It rose above the captain and above the ship like a huge fan, then crashed into the water. Each time the tail smashed into the water our ship burst into the air and came down against the hard sea. The captain looked like a little doll standing before the gigantic tail.

"Behind you!" I yelled to the captain. "Behind you!"

"Exactly, my girl. Keep the wind behind you and sail straight ahead. Keep your sights before you!"

"But the whale! There is a whale behind you!"

I struggled to my feet, waved my arms, jumped and screamed, and finally persuaded the captain to turn around. When he did, he took one look at the giant tail, turned back toward me, and fainted.

The wheel, once again, spun freely around and around. The ship was tossed up into the air. The giant tail rose and fell. I was thrown to the deck, then I bumped my head on a hard piece of wood. The last thing I remembered seeing before blacking out was Trab running toward the stern.

11

A Bump on the Head

At first I could barely open my eyes, not because of the bump, or because of my fear, but because of a bright light that turned out to be the full sun tacked upon a clear blue sky. Only then did I notice that the ship was no longer moving. I was alone on the deck of a Royal Navy vessel that sat on the calm waters of a peaceful round bay.

I ran to the wheel, hoping to see the captain, but he was not there. The wheel had been secured with a rope, the sails were properly trimmed, and the flag was still waving at the top of the mast, so I figured there was no immediate danger.

"The whale," I said in a whisper.

I ran past the wheel and to the very edge of the deck, but I was afraid to look over the railing. When I finally gained the courage to do so, all I could see were the calm blue waters reflecting fragments of sunlight.

I turned from the railing and called out, "Trab!" Then I ran the full length of the ship to the bow. "Trab!" I called again.

The ship was pointing toward a distant shore: a white beach lined with thick green trees.

"Trab!" No answer. I was alone.

Until then, I had never heard my own heartbeat. Now it felt like an ache, as if something was breaking inside me. There was so much all at once: the sudden storm, the sudden calm. I had never felt violence and calm so close together as I did on that day, nor did either part ever strike me so hard. I had never felt so much the pain of being in the middle of things, except maybe on the day my mother died.

12

Gentle Friend

his was the time to cry, and I fully intended to do so, when out to my right, upon the flat sea, a churning, bubbling, and hissing sound split the silence as a spray of water ten trees high shot up in one powerful explosion and rushed toward the sky.

I watched this geyser for a moment, then I saw the water under the fountain slowly turn from blue to gray until the enormous whale rose gently to the surface so as not to rock the ship.

"So, I didn't dream you up!" I was not afraid.

The whale swam around the ship as I ran from rail to rail, stern to bow, port to starboard. I followed her as she drew her tail from the water, letting it slide back and forth like a fern in the wind.

"Hello!" I called out, waving. "Hello!" And the whale blew another stream of water up into the sky.

"You saved us from the storm, didn't you? You carried us on your back!" Again, the geyser blew in response.

"Well," I called out over the deep water, "I'd like to thank you!" This time there was no answer.

Having no one else, I asked the whale, "What do I do now?"

The gentle whale rolled over on her back, then returned to her belly. She looked at me. I looked at her. She smiled, struck her great tail into the water, rose once like a dancer, then dove.

I never saw the whale again, but her final dive stirred the ocean floor, releasing a large pink shell, which rose to the surface and gently bumped against the side of the ship.

I watched the narrow plank I had used to board the ship extend itself from the deck and down into the wide-open shell. As I looked around, I saw this was my best invitation, so I found my roller skates, stepped over the railing, and slid down the plank.

13

Pink Shell

From what I had learned in books, I guessed my shell was a scallop, but this one was huge. I could stand in its center as if I were in a steady raft; I could sprawl in it without touching either end with my head or feet.

The shell carried me closer and closer to the white shore. I didn't know how it moved. I know the moon can pull the tides upon a beach; I know the strength of the wind, but I don't know what pressed me right and left and what kept me from tipping. I could smell flowers, a sure sign I was approaching land, or, at least, a place of fancy.

I turned around to look back at the ship, longing for a hint about my possible return home, but it was gone. I wondered how things appeared and disappeared so quickly without my help. The world is a fast place.

My shell began to slow her speed. The shoreline was straight. The trees looked peaceful. What I didn't like was the thin column of gray smoke that rose from somewhere deep within the jungle.

I felt the bottom of the shell brush lightly against the lip of the beach. I stepped out of the sea and onto the land. The sudden fresh air no longer had the smell of salt, but just the scent of flowers and rocks and trees, about the same as the park at home, but heavier.

A soft foam rose under the large pink shell as it slowly returned to the sea, sinking under the constant surf. And, like everything else I had come across recently, the shell disappeared.

Letting go of things I liked was getting easier and easier, yet I was glad to see my roller skates on the sand. I had forgotten them in the shell, but there they were. I had stopped questioning my luck. Then I smelled smoke.

14

Jungles and Grumbles

Smoke meant fire. Fire meant one of two things: lightning; or people with matches, lighters, a camp. I hoped this particular fire had been started with a match.

I stepped into the jungle in search of the camp and information, not answers. Perhaps someone there could tell me how far it was to my back lot, to my father, to home. I did not really care to know why shells carried little girls about. I simply wanted directions home.

When I was about four, I liked to pull my sheet and blanket over my head before going to sleep. The warm layers of cloth made me feel protected against the dark. Now, as I walked deeper into the jungle, I wished I had my sheets and blankets to make me invisible.

There was a little sunlight filtering through the trees. The leaves on the giant trees were twice the size of me. I heard a low growling sound and a soft cracking of sticks and twigs. Each step I took forced my heart to beat faster.

The leaves were wet. The ground was covered with low mushrooms and moss. The more I walked, the harder it became to stay in a straight line. I had to zig and zag around thick trunks, hanging vines, and large rocks.

One moment I moved like a turtle, bending low and close to the ground, pressing my belly under drooping branches. The next moment I was tangled like a confused spider, trying to haul myself through thick vines.

I was walking through a new darkness, a sudden darkness I feared would still be there tomorrow and the next day and the next, no matter what power the sun had on everything else.

This darkness reminded me of another dream I used to have again and again when I was very small. I would be asleep in my bed when, from a distance I could not understand, a darkness would approach. Not a nightfall, not horses charging toward me, not a mask over my face, but something large like a wall, yet not a wall. It always had a voice speaking in a language I could not understand. It was a single-word language, something like a hum, but louder and certainly directed at me. Then this tall, thick shadow would fall upon me like a pair of wings.

Perhaps it was this memory that nearly

made me scream as I tripped over a stone and fell to the ground. When I looked up, I imagined I was once again under those terrible wings, which turned out to be two giant tropical leaves hovering above my head. I wished to remain on the ground. I wanted to sleep or weep when I smelled smoke again and I heard, not too far off, some type of grumbling and complaining and the ringing of a bell.

15

The Reunion

Wind and water, and now this! A fine afternoon! Bother! A fine afternoon! Wind and water! No place for me. Not at all, not at all, not at all!"

I stood up and slowly walked toward the familiar voice in the darkness. Each step brought me closer and closer to the smoke and complaints.

"Blessed with one thing; now cursed with another! Bother!"

I pressed on until, drawing back a single leaf, I saw a giant fire, and in the fire a spit, and on the spit six large potatoes. The light from the fire swept around the glade, glowed brightly against the huge body of . . . Trab as he stood adjusting the burning wood.

He was certainly my Trab, but changed. He was now nearly as tall as me.

I burst out from my hiding place with a pleased cry. "Trab!"

"What's this?" he asked, turning toward me quite without fear.

"Trab! It's me, Augusta! I thought you were lost!"

I hugged him around the waist and laughed.

"Well, yes, Augusta, a fine thing. A very fine thing to see you!" And Trab hugged me awkwardly, for of course he had never hugged me before.

16

Baked Potatoes

However did you find yourself in the middle of the jungle?" I said.

"Well," replied Trab as he sat down next to the open fire, "it was like this. When the ship began to roll on the great waves and when the wind pressed against the sails, I saw the enormous tail sticking out from the rear of the ship."

"That was my whale."

"Yes, perhaps, Augusta. I rushed past the

captain, who was sleeping flat on his back, it seemed to me; then I ran to the rail. Augusta, it was the most amazing thing for a cat to see: a fishtail twice the size of a house. I have eaten lots of fish, but I never saw anything like this. The whale was actually carrying us on its back. I was about to run and tell you there was nothing to be frightened about when I was flung into the crashing ocean, and, as you know, Augusta, I can't swim, so I was sure that was the end. I even felt it was of no use to hold my breath!"

"Trab, how many times must I tell you not to give up on things so easily?"

"Yes, yes! And this time you were right again, for the next moment I was floating in the green-blue water like a rag: loose and jellylike. I could feel the water pressing all around me; I could feel it seeping through my fur. I dared, one last time, to open my eyes when, there, in the blue, wild water, I saw charging toward me a huge darkness. I thought death was inviting me in. I kicked away under the water, but the shape advanced toward me faster and faster until I was pulled into it. That is when I thought about you, and about all your adventures, and about the stories you'd tell, and I thought how this whole trouble wouldn't have happened if you hadn't thought so hard and stirred up the dust!"

"I'm sorry, Trab."

"Oh no, that is not the trouble now. I rolled and tumbled into that darkness, certain again it was the end for me, when suddenly I popped my head up, and there I was in the strangest place I had ever been. It looked from the inside like a half-finished house: all beams and rafters exposed along the walls and ceiling. Everything felt damp. There was a heavy mist.

"Beyond the mist I saw a glass case. Inside I discovered maps: red maps, yellow maps, green maps, mostly about the seas and harbors, and there was one map that showed the way to a certain desert town that sat under a bright star of some sort. I also found a large brass compass, an anchor, a rope, and a chair, which I sat on because I was tired and confused. That is when I realized I was in the belly of the great whale."

"Did you feel as if you had been eaten?"

"Augusta! Please! I'm just getting ready for dinner!"

"Sorry."

"There was something else very strange about being inside the whale, even though that was strange enough. The tall candles on the table were lit, which allowed me to see a good distance before me. I wondered who had lit them. Sometimes it is hard to believe someone you cannot see is lighting candles for you!"

"I suppose it is."

"I was wondering about all this when

everything turned upside down, and I bumped my head on the ceiling."

"That must have been when the whale turned over on her back because I asked her a question or two," I admitted.

"So I can blame *you* for my bumps and bruises, too?"

"I guess so," I answered, wanting to laugh. "But Trab, how did you escape?"

"Escape, Augusta? I didn't escape. I was set free, or should I say I was sent by air delivery to this very spot, which, as you may see, is made of very soft grass and moss." Trab pressed his foot into the ground, which did act like a sponge.

"Trab." I smiled, half expecting him to admit he was making up the whole story.

"Augusta, I was spit out by the whale and hurled like a cannonball to this very spot!"

I just gaped at Trab as he went back to roasting potatoes.

"Oh, I believe you in a friendly sort of way," I said.

"Believe whatever you like," Trab said in a huff. "I have no proof, except that I am alone and had no other way of arriving here from that sinking ship. As you know, I cannot swim. The great whale was kind enough to keep me on my four paws just a while longer, so if you don't believe me . . ."

"Trab, it is hard to keep track of what is happening. Just look at yourself. You are nearly as tall as I am now. How do you explain that?"

"Augusta! Why must you have explanations for everything? A balloon is little. Blow enough air into it and it grows! How should I know? These things happen. Isn't it enough to just accept things! It seems to me you can believe what you see and believe what you don't see all at the same time!"

"Trab?"

"If you don't believe me, what about that key, and the peach tree, and that ship, and here's my jungle, and . . ."

"Trab, I believe you." I was trying to sound convincing.

In a near whisper Trab said, "That was a wonderful whale, wasn't it, Augusta?"

"Yes, it was," I whispered back. "Trab? Do you have any extra potatoes?"

"Help yourself. A meal divides itself when needed."

Together Trab and I sat near the fire and peeled our potatoes.

17

Vibrations

After Trab and I ate our meal and drank water from the pockets of the great leaves around us, we decided to go to sleep, for the night was upon us, and the day could not possibly squeeze out another adventure. We pressed ourselves as close to the shrinking fire as we dared. Trab curled against me in a catlike way, and even managed to purr. Then we both slept.

That night was full of sounds I had never

heard before—clicks and hoots, whispers and moans. There were shaking sounds in the bushes and rumbling sounds in the shadows.

The air moved about us with the motion of wings and leaves brushing against the trees. Trab heard nothing because he was sleeping with his paws over his ears. And in my restless sleep I thought that at any moment the noises would turn into a bear or a tiger that would fall upon us, but I woke up at dawn safe and warm, with faint sunlight pressing through the thick roof of leaves.

"It's about time you woke up," Trab said.

"What are you doing?" I asked, rubbing my eyes as I watched Trab press an ear to the ground.

"I'm listening."

"What are you listening to?"

"Vibrations." Trab liked to be mysterious sometimes. I thought he was being a pest.

"*Ssssh!*" Trab was too serious, which also annoyed me. "I think they are coming closer."

"Who?" I asked in a whisper.

"Well, I'm not quite sure. The ground is too soft for an accurate guess. There seems to be three or four approaching from the east."

"Trab," I asked, slightly worried but trying to keep my humor, "do you think we should be polite and offer them tea and biscuits?"

"Do you have tea, Augusta? I'd like a bit of that."

"Well, no, but I was wondering, if I had some should I offer it?"

"I don't think they are going to be our guests," Trab said as he stood up from the ground. "If you'll turn around slowly, Augusta, I think you will see what I mean."

Sure enough, when I did turn around I saw that we were not the ones receiving guests. We were the guests. After all, Trab and I had arrived in the jungle the night before without anybody's invitation. There we were that morning, standing in the glade before a lion, a tiger, and a panther. These were not ordinary wild cats. From the looks of things, they were not wild at all, but all very proper, dressed in formal vests, fancy hats, leather shoes, and woolen socks.

18

Three Visitors

Good morning," I said with my polite voice.

"Have you come to teach us?" the lion spoke in a roarlike manner.

"Augusta," Trab whispered beside me. "I'd watch my whiskers around this bunch."

"Have you come to bring us the knowledge?" the tiger asked, stepping forward a bit.

"Where is your bag of tricks?" asked the panther.

"My," I said. "So many questions to answer all at once. Don't you think a proper introduction should come first?"

"But we must know," said the lion, "if you have come to teach us."

"Well, no," I answered, thinking the truth might be the best answer.

"You see," Trab began as he paced back and forth, "what we have here is a puzzlement. One girl, Augusta here, and one cat, that's me, were simply playing around this old peach tree in the back lot yesterday morning."

As soon as Trab began to speak, the lion, the tiger, and the panther sat down as if expecting a lecture.

"Augusta," Trab said, turning to me, "I don't think this is a normal jungle."

As Trab and I began to whisper, the three large cats stood up. The lion spoke. "The lesson. Have you, too, prepared the lesson for us?"

"What do you mean 'too'?" I asked.

"Have you come to take her place?" the tiger continued.

"Whose place?" I asked.

"Hildamore's," the panther whispered. "Hildamore's."

19

Fears and Rumors

I looked at Trab. He did not know any more than I did. "And who is this Hildamore?" I said.

"Oh," the lion answered with less and less courage. "It is true she once had long hair like you, and a soft face, but now she carries a wooden look about her, something hard, stiff, and old."

"And she makes us repeat and recite over and over again . . . words, songs, and more words and more songs." The panther turned his eyes away from me.

"And she could lift us all with one hand if she wished, or blow down the entire jungle with one breath, and pick out our eyes with one snap of her fingers. She can do these things and more." When the tiger finished speaking, he looked at me as if I had an answer waiting for him.

"When did she come here?" I asked.

"She has been here since the first rains," the tiger answered.

"Well," Trab said with obvious impatience, "why haven't you left?"

"Hildamore," said the lion.

"Hildamore," said the tiger.

"Yes, yes, yes," Trab answered, "but why haven't you simply hopped on your imagination and run?"

"We belong to her," the panther said.

"Well," Trab continued, "if I lived in a house where mice were few and the fire was usually out, I'd simply flick my tail, jump down the steps, run through the lane, and dash off to a comfortable park, or fish market, or farmyard."

"But Hildamore," the lion whispered once more.

"Trab, do you think we could help them escape?" I was willing to try.

"Augusta, how often should you interfere in other people's business?"

"Isn't there a difference between interfering and kindness?"

"Well, I suppose so, but there hasn't been a Hildamore in our neighborhood, Augusta. What do you plan to do about her?"

"Well," I said, as if I had a plan, "we'll just have to go off and see her about all this."

Trab looked at me, sighed, and then sat down to try on my roller skates.

"But we've never gone to see . . ." said the lion.

"She always comes to see us," interrupted the tiger.

"She's been known to boil strangers," whispered the panther.

I didn't like the idea of being boiled, but I also didn't like the idea of someone being so rude.

So we packed up, and one lion, one tiger, one panther, one huge cat named Trab, and I turned to the west and began our walk to the house of Hildamore.

20

Hildamore

It is easier to be afraid of things when those around you look frightened. Every time one of us stepped on a stick or kicked a stone, I or one or two of the big cats would jump up or cry out. Of course, I was not so sure of what I was supposed to be afraid. It was true that the jungle grew darker and darker the more we walked along the stone-lined path. It was also true that we were going to meet someone who, as far as I could gather, had a long nose, hair as thick as straw, and feet the size of pancakes.

"And Hildamore keeps a large glass filled with beetle shells and a jar of dried mushrooms," the lion warned. "I have heard about her collection: jars of rabbit teeth and butterfly wings; jars filled with bones and cricket legs. Augusta, you have not seen such things as we tell you. Hildamore is like no other woman you have ever met. Her power is greater than the tallest waterfall. She can reach farther than the farthest star and tap you on the shoulder. I have seen bears run wild through the raspberry fields just because they smelled that she had passed there a week before."

"Well," I said, trying to sound brave, "I am not afraid of any long-nosed jar-keeper."

At that moment there was a quick breeze that passed along our clothes and through our hair.

"You see," said the lion. "Hildamore is everywhere."

"But that is just the wind." I laughed.

"They say," the tiger whispered, "that when Hildamore breathes, she pulls all the jungle air into her lungs and blows out what she doesn't use, which is hot and steamy, and brings the morning mist upon the ground."

"How big is this Hildamore?" I asked.

"As big as a tree," said the panther.

"As big as a house," the lion corrected.

"I'd say she could not fit comfortably inside an elephant skin," the tiger said with much authority.

I was beginning to suspect something.

"When will we see Hildamore?" I asked.

"In a day."

"At least another month."

"Any minute now."

"Certainly in an hour."

"Oh, we will never arrive. Let's turn back."

Trab stepped up to me and whispered, "Augusta, I think *they're* full of hot air."

21

A Memory

When I was eight, a bit smaller than I am now, I didn't want to go into my mother's room one afternoon because there had been a fight between my mother and father. Something about not paying the rent and buying a tapestry. There was lots of loud banging of doors, and my father saying things about art and stars and being alone now and again. Then he sat down at the piano and sang a song. That is when my mother stormed around the house knocking over chairs and screaming.

I ran under the living room table and curled up deeply in the darkness there. My father's voice mixed with my mother's voice. His singing turned into yelling, and my mother must have grown to the size of a tree, or a house, or an elephant. At least her voice sounded that large. I cannot tell you how long I stayed under the table: a day? a month? a few minutes?

The house was quiet after my father slammed one more door, the door to his study, and my mother slammed the door to her room. When I finally did crawl out from under the table, I wanted to go to my mother. I even walked up to her bedroom door.

I had spent many hours in my mother's room. My mother called it her dream room. "Augusta," she'd say, "whenever you are tired, come to my dream room and see what you can find." Once I found a string of pearls in the top drawer of the dresser, and a pair of long white gloves nestled together in a box of dried flower petals. I pulled the gloves onto my hands and draped the pearls around my neck and pretended I was a queen, a dancer, my mother bowing before the mirror.

Her room always smelled of lemon, soap, and perfume. I used to pretend her small bottles of perfume were secret jewels, and I'd hide them behind the rose curtains or under the bed.

When my mother and father had their big fight, I wasn't sure if I could still go into my mother's room. I held the glass doorknob. It felt cold, like ice. I wanted to turn the handle and step in. I knew I'd find my mother on her bed with her long hair neatly combed and the lights turned low. But I also remember thinking that she might still be angry at my father or at me, and that she might have truly turned into something like stone or fire. I even thought for a moment that she might have grown thorns in her hair, and would be waiting for someone to boil.

I was ready to find another hiding place, but then I let my heart break and I turned the doorknob. I stepped in and said, "Mom?" and I ran to her as she was sitting, perfectly lovely on her bed, combing and combing her long brown hair.

She hugged me. I remember her warm arms around my shoulders as she said, "Storms rise sometimes in a house, but cannot really be explained except to say that when people live together, they bump into each other every now and again and cause a bit of thunder." She sat there for a moment, then finished, "But the rains come, and all is at peace again."

Then, as she started combing my hair, she said, "Augusta, what do we sometimes call this room?"

"Our dream room."

"Yes, my girl. And what is it on other days?"

"Just a room?"

"Yes, Augusta. Sometimes my room is a dream room, and other times it is just a room. When you are at school and you think of this room, what do you call it?"

"In my mind it is always a dream room," I answered as my mother finished combing my hair.

"See, Augusta? People remember what is special or fanciful, even when they are not right next to what they love."

I didn't see, but I remember my mother clipping a blue ribbon in my hair, which made me feel beautiful and dreamlike.

22

Screaming and Screaming

None of you has ever seen Hildamore, have you?" I finally said with conviction.

"But there was a certain night when I was nearly asleep," the lion started. "My house rocked back and forth as if it were on the sea, and, well, who else could it have been but Hildamore?"

"Silly nonsense," Trab grumbled.

"And once," said the tiger, "when I was by the river scooping out a fish from the running water, all the fish suddenly leaped out of the river and the yellow sun reflected against them and they quickly dove back into the currents. Explain that!"

"Must be Hildamore." Trab smirked. I stepped on his big tail.

"And once," the panther added, "when I was walking through the forest near the hollow trees, I heard a great hooting and puffing and blowing. Hildamore, of course. It was her to be sure."

"But," I said, as Trab licked his tail, "I read in a big book on my father's shelf that a house will rock in a dream. And you, Tiger, couldn't fish jump from the water in a friendly greeting? I saw pictures of that once. And Panther, even I have heard the melody of the woods, a one-bird whistle as the wind blows between the branches." They all looked a bit ashamed.

"Humph!" I continued. "I think you all imagined this Hildamore and made her up to be so grand and powerful that she has made you afraid of walking alone."

"Yeah," Trab added cautiously.

"Why," I continued, "I bet there isn't even anyone in this deep jungle but the three of you, and you are scaring your own shadows. And if there was such a person, I hope I would have the courage . . ."

This is where I stopped my lecture because this is where we all heard a loud, spinning shrill, a screaming, screaming, screaming.

23

Chicken Soup Song

We stood in the cement of our frozen footsteps.

"Hildamore," the lion whispered.

"I can feel her vibrations," the tiger whimpered.

"I'm beginning to itch," the panther said as he began to scratch his leg.

Two things led me to believe what they were saying. One, the wailing was a sound I had never heard before, and two, through the thick trees I could just see a tall, thin gray house with black smoke pouring out of the green chimney.

"I've never come this far," the lion admitted.

"How do you think we should approach her?" I asked. "Through the front gate? Announced? Unannounced? I could throw a pebble against the front window."

"I think," Trab said, "we should pretend we are just passing by. Let's sing and talk about chicken soup. She is bound to hear us, then it will be up to her to decide what to do."

I wanted to sing the national anthem. Trab thought it best that we sing a song about brave travelers on a pilgrimage.

While Trab and I tried to decide what song would be best, the lion, the tiger, and the panther pretended they were greatly interested in making chicken soup.

"Let the bones boil for three days," said the lion.

"Nonsense," the tiger argued. "The broth

should cook for an hour, at which time carrots and rice need be added."

"We are good at pretending, Augusta," Trab said, leading us forward.

The screaming and wailing began again and stopped our talking, and nearly sent the lion back the opposite way.

"Look brave," Trab whispered. "Let's talk louder and sing."

That is what we did until we nearly reached the property line of the tall house. I was about to sing about traveling around the world in a fancy ship when the front door opened and out stepped an old, old woman.

From a distance I could not tell if she was good or bad, but she was surely something, and she was surely waving to us, though at first I couldn't decide if she was asking us to come closer or to go away. Then the screams began again, and this time the old woman made an effort to lift her hand higher, which, finally, seemed to be a clear invitation.

24

Give Me Your Hand

Trab, Lion, Panther, and Tiger weren't sure what to do, so they just stood on the path and watched as I began to walk slowly toward the house.

As I stepped through the gate and walked up to the woman, I said, "Hello," with a bit of a curtsy. "I'm Augusta."

"Oh, I know," the old woman said. When she spoke she didn't lift her head, but rather turned her face up just a bit as if she were drinking from a fountain.

I had given up being startled when strangers knew my name.

"Are you Hildamore?" I asked, feeling a bit silly.

"Give me your hand," the old woman said.

I looked behind me to see what had become of the big cats. They stood like stones. Perhaps they were stones. Some roads are meant to be taken alone.

I offered my hand to the old woman. She placed hers into mine. Her hand was warm and wrinkled.

"In the back," the old woman said, and she began a slow walk around the thin house, leading me through a wide garden of wildflowers.

"Pickerel weed. Adder's tongue. Lady's slipper. Columbine. Indian pink. Clover."

As we passed each flower, the old woman spoke its name as if each one deserved an applause.

"Sorrel. Mallow. Queen Anne's lace. Primrose. Milkweed. Foxglove." I wondered whether she expected me to acknowledge each one with a salute.

"Mullein, Augusta, and Indian paintbrush. Ironweed. Black-eyed Susan. Chicory . . ."

"This one's yarrow!" I shouted with delight.

"Yes, Augusta, yarrow."

I was hoping to find a peach tree when, once again, that terrible, wailing scream scratched the silence.

"Ah . . ." I said with false courage, "we are travelers on a pilgrimage in search of chicken soup, and I think I must be going . . ."

"Do not be afraid, Augusta."

I looked at the old woman's dress, which hung about her like a spider's web. Her shoes were laced and tied. She didn't walk exactly, but rather pulled her feet slowly along the path.

Was this woman a servant leading me to the mad and terrible, screaming Hildamore, who was waiting behind the house in her garden of thorns? Would there be a great fire, or a tower of bones?

"Navigation, Augusta," said the old woman. "Remember, all it takes is a few careful steps."

And so I walked carefully along the flagstones one by one so as not to step on a crack or on any of the flowers. Finally we turned the corner of the house to see what I had not expected: a pig, a small pink pig the size of a loaf of bread, with its hind legs stuck in the wooden lattice of the backyard fence. The pig was screaming and wailing, wailing and screaming.

25

The Pig and the Drawings

S he is caught in the fence," the old woman said. "I could not free her leg. You came just at the right time. Won't you help?"

The woman released my hand. I approached the pig. It stopped screaming. I was able to separate the slats of wood with difficulty, and then the pig was free. It limped around the yard, curled its tail up and down, and said, "Thank you." Then the pig jumped over a high wall. I ran to the wall, peeked over the top, and watched the pig waddle down a small path toward the largest gathering of animals I have ever seen: hens and kangaroos and mice and falcons, and even giraffes and zebras, and a herd of elephants. Even the largest zoo was nothing compared with all the animals I saw stretched out to the distant mountains. There were panda bears sitting on the grass, bulls sleeping under the linden trees. Emus, water buffalo, llamas, camels! Suddenly a parrot and a collection of hummingbirds flew into the yard. A crow flew up and landed on the tilted shoulder of the old woman.

"Yes, Augusta. I am Hildamore."

When I looked at her this time, there was a collection of lines in her face that, surely, turned themselves into a smile.

"Oh, do not be surprised," she said in answer to my question-mark face.

"I am a little. They told me you were someone to be afraid of."

"I am to those who are lost," Hildamore

said as she sat upon a wood bench along a little hedge. "Come next to me, Augusta."

I was still afraid, but her voice sounded familiar in a distant sort of way.

As we sat, a llama walked up to Hildamore and blinked once, then again.

"Yes," Hildamore continued. "Those who are lost fear me."

It seemed as if the llama was speaking to Hildamore, yet I didn't hear any words spoken between them. Hildamore did eventually nod her head slowly up and down, and the llama walked away.

"You see, Augusta, I have been keeping track."

She took a stick from the ground and began to draw several lines in the soft dirt at our feet.

"This line is the river. On this side of the shore there was nothing. On this side, where we are today, there was great confusion."

Hildamore drew elephants and birds and

snakes and lions scattered here and there among trees and tall grasses. Some of the animals were drawn standing on their heads. Fish were against the rocks, and mice were at the bottom of the river.

"Long before people entered the jungle, the animals were forgetting who they were. I arrived much the same way you did, upon a pink shell. Someday your daughters will know the feel of pearl upon their feet.

"You see, Augusta, coming completely out of the sea as we have done did not prepare us for the world. We have smooth curves. The world is very sharp and crooked. We need to be protected."

"I know," I said. "My house is square on a square street with jagged fences and crooked windows. And sometimes when I walk in the rain my father lifts his jacket over my head or pops out his umbrella, but I like to get wet."

"These are little things. You are really too

young to know yet exactly what I mean, but you are well on your way."

I was offended. After all, I had survived a dark storm upon the wild sea. I had a commission from the queen.

"Here, Augusta. Look here."

Again Hildamore began to draw in the dirt. "This is where you are now. You still must travel along this line until you arrive here."

She drew an *X* upon the earth.

"What will this place look like? How will I recognize that I have arrived?"

Hildamore stood up and extended her thin arm, and again she led me. This time we walked quickly through the garden to a side door and into her tall, thin house.

26

Matching

We entered a room to the left, a room like none I had ever seen. On one wall, thin glass shelves reached up twenty feet from the floor to the ceiling. Against the other wall sat an equal-sized shelf filled with books: fat books, skinny books, tall books, and short books. From the floor to the ceiling they rose up like bricks. There were books for children and books for mothers. There were father books and medicine

books, star books and butterfly books. I saw
books about acorns and books about rivers.

"This is where I do my matching,"
Hildamore whispered.

"Matching?" I asked.

"When a zebra forgets that it is a zebra,
and it no longer knows what to do, it
comes to me and I teach it the difference
between stripes and solid colors. I bring it
to the veldts and let the wind brush against
its face. Soon the zebra knows again that it
is not an elephant or an antelope, but a
zebra. I must do lots of reading to learn all
there is to learn about the zebra, so I spend
much time on this side of my room, taking
down this book or that book until I am
sure the inside of me knows what I am
seeking. But the outside, Augusta. We must
match what we feel on the inside with
those things on the outside. So I go to the
other side of the room, to these glass
shelves where I keep all my glass jars. In

these jars I have bits and pieces of every-thing. It has taken me many years to gather this collection. Let me show you."

Hildamore walked to her glass jars. Thousands of them were carefully placed upon the glass shelves.

"Let me see. Wax. Water. Zipper. Zinnia. Here, zebra."

Hildamore brought down a small jar, about the size of a light bulb, and inside the jar I saw a few coarse hairs, thin black-and-white hairs. Zebra.

"If a mushroom finds itself with wings," Hildamore explained, "and beats against the porch light at night like a crazy moth, I go to my books and read and read about mush-rooms. Then I come to my jars. Look here."

Hildamore reached up and brought to me the jar marked MUSHROOM.

"Open it, Augusta."

I did.

"Spores, Augusta. Take one out."

I did that, too.

"Now spit upon it."

I am not the type of girl who spits, but just the same I spat on the yellow spot in my hand, and, slowly, a mushroom puffed its way up on my open palm.

"You see, Augusta. Mushroom! And my little friend is no longer confused, so she drops the wings and tiptoes back to her moist place in the woods."

I wasn't quite sure that I did see, but it did seem that for each problem, Hildamore had an answer by matching her books with her glass jars. She explained how one day a rooster was sitting in the corner of the yard feeling useless and hateful, so he fell before Hildamore's feet as she walked by.

The rooster cried out that he was nothing but feathers and bones. Hildamore took the rooster to her matching room and looked up "rooster" in her library. The rooster sat beside her as Hildamore read about mornings and barnyards. Already the rooster was feeling more hopeful. Hildamore then took the rooster to the jar collection on the other side of the room and pulled down a jar that held six small red feathers. Hildamore shook the feathers in the jar, and they wiggled back and forth against the glass walls. She took one feather out of the jar and sewed it to the chest of the lost rooster. The rooster knew who he was again, and this made him happy.

"Ever since," Hildamore explained, "that rooster climbs upon the shoulder of the yard each morning and cock-a-doodle-doos the sun right up into the sky."

"This is wonderful," I said. "Then all the animals in your backyard have come because they have forgotten who they are?"

"Yes," Hildamore said.

"And you match their insides and their outsides with your books and glass jars?"

"Yes," Hildamore whispered.

"And the lion and the tiger and the panther who came with me are really coming to see you to find out who they are?"

"Yes."

"You can remind a rooster or a snail or a bear where they belong?"

Again Hildamore whispered, "Yes."

Then it was my turn to whisper. "What about me?"

"Are you lost, Augusta?"

"Well, something doesn't seem right inside," I answered. "But I am brave. I can stand on a ship in a nasty storm. I am willing to slide into strange pink shells. I can walk through dark shadows, under thick vines, and upon green moss. But sometimes I feel as if I am just a broken leaf floating from a branch in autumn. I feel like an icicle fallen from the eaves of a roof. I feel as if I am a lost balloon carried away wherever the wind chooses."

"When did you first feel these things?" Hildamore asked.

"I think," I said, holding tightly to my roller skates, "when my mother died."

"Come, Augusta. Let's see what my books and jars say about lost girls."

27

The Book

Hildamore led me to the wall of books as if she were selecting a new dress for me. She hummed and said "yes" and "no," and she hummed some more as she looked at the books to our right and at the books to our left.

If I were to select the book, I thought, I would take the thin one with the green cover. It looked new and fancy. That is how I wished to be: new and fancy. And if a book can give an idea as to what I am, well, I thought, that *was* the book to read.

Instead, after much hesitation, which worried me a bit, Hildamore reached to the far left for a fat, old book that didn't look promising. The book seemed to rest like a pillow in Hildamore's arms as she slowly walked to the one chair that stood in the center of the room.

"Come with me, Augusta."

I was surprised when Hildamore instructed me to sit in the large blue chair. My feet didn't reach the floor when I sat.

Hildamore placed the large book upon my lap. It didn't feel heavy.

"Now," she continued, "turn some pages slowly, and I will point out a few lines for you to read aloud. Just begin anywhere."

So I bent over the book as if I were looking for a telephone number, and flipped the pages here and there. Hildamore leaned over my shoulder and ran her crooked finger along one page until she stopped at a line. "Read."

"'Love is strong as death,'" I read.

"And now here," Hildamore continued, pointing at another line. So again I read.

"'Your mother raised you up under the apple tree.'" But I didn't understand.

"Read," Hildamore answered with another pointing of her finger.

"'Who is this that comes up from the wilderness?'" Then I asked, "Me?"

Hildamore nodded with a smile. "Here, Augusta. Read here."

"'Many waters cannot quench love,'" and then I thought about the sea and the pink shell and the rain I like to walk under without an umbrella.

"And here, Augusta."

"'Awake, O north wind; and come, blow upon my garden,'" and I thought about the yarrow that Trab and I picked so long ago.

"Augusta."

"'The flowers appear on the earth; the time of the singing of birds is come, and the voice of the turtle is heard in our land.'"

"It will all be of use to you someday, Augusta. Now read here."

"'I am the rose of Sharon and the lily of the valley.' I like that," I said.

"And now you may close the book, Augusta, and we will see if we cannot match all this with my glass jars. Come."

28

Potpourri

I wanted to read more in the old book, but Hildamore was already standing before the wall of jars, and she was humming again. I hopped off the chair, placed the book where I had been sitting, and walked quietly to Hildamore's side.

"Somewhere here there is a positive match. Can you see it, Augusta?"

I looked at the many jars. Some were filled with sand and others with teeth. Some had plain water or snowflakes. Up and down the shelves I looked. There was a jar filled with rabbit fur and one filled with apple seeds. There were thousands of jars sitting on the tall shelves. I tipped my head way back to see the jars at the very top, those filled with dew and mist.

As I was trying to steady myself, I brushed against the shelf and nearly knocked down one of the jars.

"Yes, Augusta. That's it. The one by your hand. The very one I was looking for. The match."

I picked the jar off the shelf and held it up to the light. I was disappointed to see nothing in it except a collection of drab dried leaves.

"Open it, Augusta."

And so I opened it to discover, much to my delight, a perfume smell that I recognized. "Flowers, Hildamore. Flowers?"

"Yes, Augusta. Flowers. Potpourri. These

flowers have been collected each spring for many years," Hildamore explained, though she really didn't have to say much more for I was slowly beginning to understand something.

"You see, Augusta, you are the sister of the daffodils, climber of maples. The world still curves your way. There is time, my girl, there is time. We have made the match, Augusta. We have made the match."

And then I knew who I was all over again, and where I belonged, and that my mother, like the dried flowers, still had, and would always have, the power to make the air around me smell sweet. You see? There is a forever, not a maybe, or a brief visit, but a forever Sunday with mothers and fathers and aunts in long dresses and cheesecake and apple juice, a forever place.

"Hildamore, I want to go home."

"Yes, Augusta. The dust is beginning to settle. The river, travel along the river with new courage. It is waiting for you."

Hildamore led me out of the house, past

the animals in the yard, through the flower garden, and back around to the front of her house.

"Just around the corner, Augusta. Just around the corner."

"Good-bye," I called back over my shoulder as I ran quickly on my way. "Good-bye!"

I was nearly to the road when Hildamore called me back in a loud voice. "Augusta! Augusta! Your skates! You forgot your roller skates!" And there she stood before her tall house, clapping the roller skates above her head.

I ran back to her, and as she handed me the skates I stopped breathing for just a moment, kissed her lightly on the cheek, and whispered, "Thank you."

"Yes, Augusta. Yes, my girl. Be off now and bloom."

So down the path I ran, waving back again and again toward Hildamore as she, too, waved, and then I stepped around the corner into my final adventure.

29

The Useless Shipbuilders

found Trab sitting on the road playing jacks with the lion, the panther, and the tiger.

"It's your turn," I said to the wildcats.

"But it's my turn," Trab said. "They dropped the ball."

"No. Not the game, Trab. Hildamore is waiting for Lion, Panther, and Tiger. She will see them now."

"Oh!" groaned the lion.

"Oh my," said the tiger.

"Does it hurt?" the panther asked.

"Not a bit," I said. "There is a little dizziness, and wonderful smells and sounds, and there are lots of books and jars, and there is a little stretching inside of you." And before I could go on explaining, the three cats stood up, roared and purred, and threw their fancy clothes upon the ground. Then they locked arms and laughed and laughed as they walked toward Hildamore's house.

"I never could understand them," Trab said, taking one last turn with the jacks, gathering them all in a final victory. "They kept trying to tell me they were kings or something. Strange trio. So, did you like Hildamore, Augusta?"

"Yes. And she has fantastic shelves in her house."

"But of course," Trab said with a yawn.

"How do you know, Trab? And how come you don't have to see Hildamore?"

"Augusta, I keep my back against the wall and just concern myself with what quickly runs by. Things keep in order that way for me. And if you really want to know, I happen to have superior intelligence, which is a direct result of . . ."

"Trab? Do you hear anything?" I asked.

"Well, by now I am good at recognizing my heart beating. It has made lots of noise these past few days."

"I think I hear the river," I said.

"Yes. I can smell the water, too. There, just beyond the grass," Trab indicated with his right paw.

Trab and I began to run. We skipped and jumped, suddenly feeling a new freedom beyond the dark jungle. Here the land turned flat and green. The light was bright, the grass was smooth. Then we were standing along the bank of a large, powerful river. The water was white as it rushed and curled and crashed against itself.

"How can we possibly travel down this river?" I cried. "It is too fast, too deep, and we haven't a boat."

I was ready to weep when I noticed Trab gathering long strands of dry reeds that lined the shore.

"By now, Augusta, we haven't the right to moan about each little setback. Action is called for, and action I plan."

"What are you doing with the grass?" I asked Trab.

"A raft. I plan to weave a sturdy raft. Come, Augusta, I'll show you how. It is all in the planning and doing."

So Trab and I pulled at the reeds and laid them upon the dry bank.

"I've heard," said Trab, "from my grandfather about a group of ancient cats who lived in a place called Egypt. These ancestors spoke of men building ships from the river reeds. So I suspect we can build such a boat, or, maybe, a smaller version."

After we gathered what surely seemed to be enough grass, Trab and I sat before the heap and we both spoke at the same time, "Now what?"

Trab took two reeds and tried to lace them together, but the strands simply fell between his paws, and then I thought I heard low laughter.

I tried to braid three pieces, but my grass, too, fell between my fingers, and again I heard laughter, but this time it was deeper.

"Trab. I do not think we are alone."

"Augusta, don't be silly. We cannot possibly be bothered again by anyone after all we've gone through. We have a right to be left alone."

Again Trab made a weak attempt at lashing the reeds together, and again there was laughter, even louder and deeper, until there was a chorus of laughter: one small, one middle-sized, and one very large laugh.

30

The Useful Shipbuilders

I do hope you've brought your sewing needles," a small spider called up from between two blades of tall grass.

"You must understand the texture of the material," a robin said in a scolding manner from a tree branch.

"Each piece must fit just so," a fat beaver said, shaking the water from his brown coat as he stepped out from the river.

"And I," said Trab, "am more prepared to

return to being a simple house cat, Augusta, than to be subjected to a constant parade of experts."

By now it was an ordinary thing to be approached by talking animals. I would have been more startled if a boy or a baker or a woodsman had stepped out upon the trail and greeted me in a civil manner. But a spider, a robin, and a beaver speaking, that was the ordinary thing.

"Could you help us build a raft?" I asked the spider.

"Oh yes," she answered, clicking her legs every which way. "I was born to connect loose strands." And with that she set upon our pile of grass as if she had been hired at a great salary.

"And you, Robin. Do you have a suggestion?"

"Of course, though my talents are limited. I do not work at my weaving on a constant basis, but I have developed a few techniques which may be of service to you." So the robin set upon the pile of reeds and began to lace and weave one piece into another.

"Ah, you don't have to ask me, Augusta. I have come without any intentions but to help where I can." So the beaver carried large sticks and began to build a frame that slowly began to look like a splendid raft, not a ship but a flat-bottomed float.

In a very little time the raft was complete. I especially liked the two little seats in the back. Trab and I dropped the raft into the water. I was turning to thank the builders when I stopped and asked, "Where have they gone?" All I saw was a small, small spider disappearing in the grass, a bird flying up into the distance, and the water parting as the beaver slapped his tail and was gone.

"Thank you just the same," I shouted.

"Augusta. Let's be gone. I cannot hold the raft much longer. The current is too strong."

31

Downriver

The raft was strong and willing; the river was swift and deep. Trab and I had no control. We simply floated down where the water led us.

But then, "Trab," I said with a new concern.

At that moment, Trab left his little seat and stood in the very front of the raft. He couldn't hear me, or he chose not to hear me.

"Trab! We are picking up speed!"

I, too, left my seat and I joined Trab. He turned and smiled. "Augusta, do you feel the wind? Have you noticed the change? The colors? The sounds?"

So I knew Trab felt what I felt. Things were changing all around us. It was something like the sun rising in the morning. We began to pick up more speed, and more speed. The riverbanks, the trees, the sky all began to rush by us in one blend of color.

"I think we are headed in the right direction," Trab called to me, as I grabbed the side of the raft.

The raft spun around and around. The water roared. The light was bright. The air seemed thinner. I was about to fall, or cry, or laugh when there was one last, final jump and splash, then the raft nearly stopped.

We pressed our way slowly through the mouth of the river, and found ourselves suddenly upon a canal lined with bricks on either side.

Then, much like the shell I had ridden so long ago, the raft led Trab and me to a certain spot. Stone steps had been cut into the brick wall. The raft stopped at the last step. Trab, without hesitation, jumped from the raft, ran up to the top of the stairs, and disappeared.

I looked at the raft, at the water, at the light, then I slowly decided, once more, to step out of what I had come to know and into something I was not so sure about.

32

Rain

I held my skates as I walked off the steady raft. The steps were beautiful: smooth, white, long. I remembered seeing such stairs at the library and at the post office, and at school, but here, at the edge of a canal, they looked more wonderful.

I walked up one step at a time. The closer I drew to the top, the more I saw what was laid out before me: trees, grass, flowers. Then I heard, from a great distance, "Augusta! Augusta!"

I climbed to the top of the stairs.

"Augusta!" the faraway voice continued.

Trab, I thought. I began to run.

"Augusta! Augusta!"

I ran through a park, past an empty fountain. I ran and I ran. After a loud, sudden rumble, I dropped one of my skates, and then I ran some more toward the voice.

"Augusta!"

Suddenly, dust from the path began to whirl about my feet, my legs, my arms, my face. The wind. The wind. Some leaves broke free from their branches. The dust pressed into my eyes. I couldn't see, but I could still hear my name being called. The closer I ran toward the voice, the farther away it seemed to be. The dust boiled and blew faster and thicker.

"Augusta! Augusta! Augusta!"

Once again I was afraid for Trab. Then it began to rain. First a few drops, then a few more, then a rush of water . . . a downpour. The water clicked and ticked on the leaves, on my shoes, on the path. It ran through my hair, along my arms and legs, and down upon the sinking dust.

"Augusta!" I heard one more time, and then I tripped over a broom and cut my knee. I know I wanted to cry because of the pain in my leg, but I cried instead for reasons I still cannot describe, and I held my eyes tightly shut.

"Augusta. What are you doing in this rain? Come, my girl."

When I opened my eyes, I saw Trab in correct proportion to everything else, and then I saw my father as he walked steadily toward me with his wide umbrella over his head.

"Augusta! It's pouring rain!"

I closed my eyes for a second, expecting to see a ship, or a tall, thin house, or a tiger, but when I opened them again, I saw tall gray buildings on all sides of me. I was home. I liked my father's arms around me as he bent over and picked me up.

"I'm sorry I'm so late from work. The

office was filled with sick animals. My schedule was not matching my plan for the day, and I simply had to straighten things out."

"Me, too," I said.

"Augusta. How many times must I remind you to wear your slicker when you go off in the rain? At least take the extra umbrella in the hall closet."

I held on to my father's neck as he carried me back across the vacant lot. As we reached the house, he kicked open the back door, and, just before the door closed behind us, Trab shot through the remaining crack, hopped on the kitchen table, and meowed once.

My father stooped down, helped me into a kitchen chair, shook his umbrella, placed it in the umbrella stand, then said, "Let's have a look at your leg, Augusta."

"I'm all right, Daddy. I just tripped on the broom. I'm all right, really. Just a small bandage will do. I'll get one after I feed Trab."

"You sure now?"

"Yes, I'm quite sure."

"Just the same, you look in a bit of pain or something."

"Oh, I just lost one of my roller skates in the back lot somewhere."

"It will turn up," my father reassured me. "No one wants a single skate. The match is what makes them of any use to someone."

"I love you, Daddy."

"Yes, well, that makes the difference."

He hugged me and I hugged him, and Trab meowed loudly for his supper, which he was promptly given, after which my father and I had pot roast with lots of baked potatoes.

33

A Promise

After the dishes were washed and dried and put away, we walked into the living room where Trab was already curled up on the couch fast asleep.

"What will it be tonight?" my father asked as he looked up and down at his tall bookcase. "Adventure? Romance? Comedy? Poetry?"

"Poetry," I said, so poetry it was.

Each night, before I went to bed, my

father and I took turns reading aloud from a book the other person selected. That night it was my turn to choose, and my father's turn to read.

"I'd like the thin green book," I said with a yawn.

He reached for the book as I sat down on the soft old chair next to the fireplace, opposite my father, and he began to read:

Little girl,
don't eat the icicles
that hang like tassels
from the tree.

Soon you shall return to the meadow:
Its green slopes shall roll
under your feet, return to you
from winter lands, reborn.
Soon you shall become
sister of the daffodils,
climber of maples.

Soon enough you shall grow
into the tremendous flower
of your own flowering beauty

of slender womanhood.
Wait now, milk-fed little girl:
There is time enough to bite the icicles
off the tree of life
with strong young teeth.
The world still curves your way,
to your shape, and its sound
is still simple—single—
a one-bird whistle
in a musical wood.

The fire cracked and popped. Trab's bell jingled softly as he lifted his head to look at me once with a blink, then he returned to his slumber.

My father continued to read other poems that are lost to me now because I fell asleep in the chair dreaming, dreaming, dreaming.

I'd like to tell you I woke up the next day to find a beautiful peach tree growing between the cracks in the cement of the back lot, but there was just another bit of yarrow leaning slightly in the wind. No matter, for I walked out in my red pajamas, bent over the flower, and picked its white petals one by one. When I returned to the kitchen I found an empty glass jar, a jam jar with a lid.

I dropped the petals into the jar, and I watched them flutter down and cover the glass bottom with a soft cream color, then I closed the lid tightly.

I promised myself that every year I would gather the petals from the yard and keep them here beside me through the summer, fall, and winter, keep the fragrance, believing, for certain now, that spring would forever break out between the cracks of old cement.